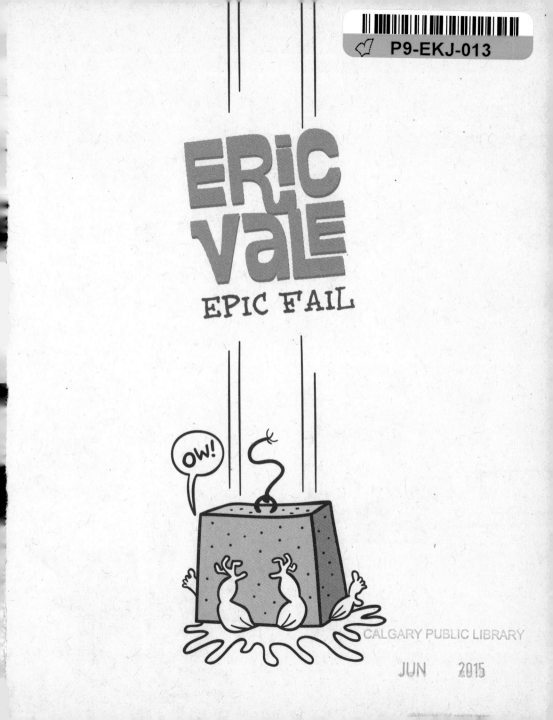

ERIC VALE

EPIC FAIL

MICHAEL GERARD BAUER

Illustrated by Joe Bauer

I HEARTILY ENDORSE THIS BOOK

Scholastic Canada Ltd.
Toronto New York London Auckland Sydney
Mexico City New Delhi Hong Kong Buenos Aires

Scholastic Canada Ltd.
604 King Street West, Toronto, Ontario M5V 1E1, Canada
Scholastic Inc.
557 Broadway, New York, NY 10012, USA
Scholastic Australia Pty Limited
PO Box 579, Gosford, NSW 2250, Australia
Scholastic New Zealand Limited
Private Bag 94407, Botany, Manukau 2163, New Zealand
Scholastic Children's Books
Euston House, 24 Eversholt Street, London NW1 1DB, UK

www.scholastic.ca

Library and Archives Canada Cataloguing in Publication

Bauer, Michael Gerard, 1955–, author
Eric Vale, epic fail / Michael Gerard Bauer ; illustrated by
Joe Bauer.
Originally published: Parkside, S. Aust. : Omnibus Books, 2012.
ISBN 978-1-4431-3925-0 (pbk.)
I. Bauer, Joe (Illustrator), illustrator II. Title.
PZ7.B322Ere 2015   j823'.92   C2014-904570-0

First published by Scholastic Australia in 2012.
This edition published by Scholastic Canada Ltd. in 2015.

6 5 4 3 2 1   Printed in Canada 139   15 16 17 18 19

For Meg who pointed out my "eric fail" – MGB
For Rita and all the hugs between the pages – JB

Epic Fail No. 1: My Nickname

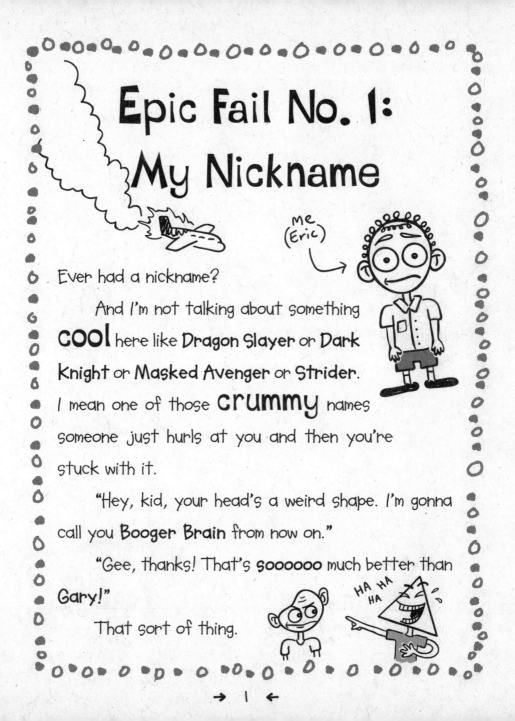

me (Eric)

Ever had a nickname?

And I'm not talking about something **cool** here like **Dragon Slayer** or **Dark Knight** or **Masked Avenger** or **Strider**. I mean one of those **crummy** names someone just hurls at you and then you're stuck with it.

"Hey, kid, your head's a weird shape. I'm gonna call you **Booger Brain** from now on."

"Gee, thanks! That's **soooooo** much better than Gary!"

That sort of thing.

HA HA HA

The problem with most nicknames is you hardly ever get to choose the one you want. Just look at what happened to Cooper King last year in Year Four. He's got this pretty good name, right, but then one day he turns up here at good old Moreton Hill Primary School and sits down in class same as normal – and **everything** changes.

First up, Martin Fassbender, who's sitting right behind him, lets out a moan like he's just seen his own face in the mirror, and the next thing you know everyone around Cooper goes **crazy**. Some kids are choking and gulping for air. Other kids are holding their breath and **turning blue**.

Most of the girls look like they're going to pass out or **throw up!**

And it's all because there's this **killer pong** coming from Cooper King and that's because Cooper's stepped on a giant piece of doggie-doo on the way to school and it's still plastered under one of his shoes like a squashed brown sausage, only he doesn't know it. Anyway, now he can forget all about being good old "Cooper King" any more, because somewhere

in Martin Fassbender's **twisted brain** a nickname has already popped up.

And **TAAA-DAAA!**

Just like magic, Cooper King changes into ...

Air Freshener

KING PONG!

Now whenever there's a whiff of something in the classroom that smells like a giant rat has **died** while gagging on a skunk in a sewer (but which is probably just Pete Bunter doing his "thing"), Martin or someone else just has to shout out, "Oh, no! Run for your lives! It's **KING PONG** and his killer POO SHOE!"

Which was probably **funny** for the first twenty or thirty times it happened. Unless you're Cooper King.

See what I mean? Nicknames can be deadly. And not in a good way. Sean Nottingham would agree. **His luck ran out** when someone saw his name on a class list shortened to **S. Nott.**

Ladies and gentlemen, give it up for Snotty Nottingham! **Ouch.**

Of course I guess you can be lucky. Some kids have pretty good nicknames. Like Tyler Webb gets to be called "Spider," which is kind of cool, and "Micky" Micareeno (who no one calls "Charles" even though that's his real name)

S. Nott. ✓
F. Lem. ✓
B. Ooga. ✓
M. Ukas ✓
N. Ostril. ✓

"Spider"? I don't get it.

and Robert Falou, who gets "Big Bob" because he's ... well ... big.

And then there's my best friend, William Rodriguez. His nickname is embarrassing enough, but the way he got it is even more embarrassing.

That happened way back one day in Year Three when we were doing this class crossword puzzle on Types of Transportation. Our teacher, Miss Wu, was checking the answers and she says, "Who thinks they have the correct answer to three across? It has seven letters and means a type of train that carries cargo? A something train."

Of course the answer Miss Wu was looking for was "freight" but for some reason William sticks his hand up and calls out, "Choo—Choo, Miss!"

Have you met my crazy, best friend Choo—Choo Rodriguez? Chewy for short.

But seriously, "Choo—Choo" train? What was he **thinking?** That he was back in kindy or something? I suppose if the clue was **People drive these on roads** his answer would have been "Brm—brms."

But wait, it gets even crazier. William actually **likes** his nickname!

I'm not kidding. He reckons that Choo—Choo Rodriguez has "a nice ring to it." Chewy's a bit weird like that.

B
R
m
B
R
m
S

He thinks **everything** is pretty good. I blame his parents. They're nice people, but they're both life coaches. I'm not sure **exactly** what that means, but they go around saying stuff like, "If you think you **can't, you won't!** If you think you **can, you will!**" and "There's no such thing as **failure,** just **delayed success!**" They've even written books — POSITIVE Thinking for POSITIVE Results! and POSITIVE Advice for the POSITIVE Family!

Chewy's mum and dad are positively **positive!** about a lot of stuff. So's Chewy. Including his **stupid** nickname.

GET DOWN AND GIVE ME CHILDHOOD!

Life Coach

But this isn't about Chewy and his stupid nickname. It's about me and my stupid nickname. Once I used to be just plain old boring ERIC VALE. And that was totally **fine** by me. I didn't want a nickname. But then one day, just like Cooper King, I got one anyway. And it ended up being way **worse** than Choo—Choo or Snotty or King Pong or even Booger Brain.

Yep, no doubt about it. My nickname was an **epic fail!**

o●o○o●o○o●o○o●o○o●o

I got my nickname the first day back after the holidays. And it was all because of Secret Agent Derek "Danger" Dale.

Here's what happened. Mr. Winter, our Year Five teacher, was out the front of the class and he was **going on** about something or other. Mum reckons Mr. Winter is "a lovely young man with the patience of a saint." I think she's got him mixed up with someone else. **Except** I guess Mr. Winter is pretty hard to miss. He's really tall and skinny and he's got this **weird** red hair. He'd make a good **traffic light.** Only it would be stuck on STOP all the time.

So anyway, while Mr. Winter was up the front of the class, I was down the back

Mr. Winter

minding my own business and looking through my **Awesome Stories and Genius Thoughts Journal.** That's a journal where I keep all my **awesome** stories and **genius** thoughts. So far I haven't had that many genius thoughts. Or any. But don't worry. I've left heaps of blank pages just in case!

But I did have lots of awesome action-adventure stories. The one I was working on that day was my **best** one ever. It was called **The Totally Awesome Action Adventures of Secret Agent Derek "Danger" Dale.** I'd just started reading over the stuff I'd written in the holidays. I was up to a really good bit. That's because Secret Agent Derek "Danger" Dale was in **big trouble...**

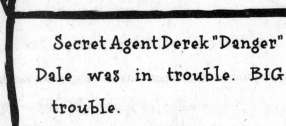

Secret Agent Derek "Danger" Dale was in trouble. BIG trouble.

See, told ya!

He was surrounded by a hundred bloodthirsty ninja assassins. They were heavily armed. They were also heavily legged and heavily stomached. Let's face it: they were just really, really fat. It was like an episode of Ninja Biggest Loser. Oh, and they had heaps of weapons too!

Pretty **exciting,** huh? But wait, it gets even better!

It was looking very bad for Secret Agent Dale. And the fact that he was handcuffed and about to be pushed off a high plank into a pool full of hungry crocs, deadly piranha and poisonous sea snakes didn't help that much either.

And neither did being naked except for a pair of old Batman undies. Old Batman undies that hadn't been changed for a month. And had holes in them. Heaps of holes. Holes in very embarrassing places. More holes than actual undies.

No doubt about it, Danger was in a wHOLE lot of trouble!

I was **on fire!** I was going to try to do a big sketch of that last scene during the holidays, but when I told Chewy, he said he'd do it for me.

Chewy's mum and dad reckon he has a "special gift" when it comes to art.

I'm not so sure.

But anyway, Mr. Winter was **still** going on about something or other out the front of the class so I kept reading.

© William C.C. Rodriguez

The narrow plank Derek was balancing on began to creak and bend. Five metres below him, the water was thrashing with starving and deadly flesh-eating monsters. The point of a ninja sword stabbed into Derek's back, pushing him even further forward.

Then an angry voice shouted at him ...

"Eric Vale! Concentrate!"

"Huh? What? Oh, yeah, yeah, I am, Mr. Ninja – aaah, I mean Whinger – I mean Winter!"

For some reason Mr. Winter was giving me a bit of a **Death Stare**.

I thought I'd better concentrate like he said. So I tried. I really did. But it wasn't easy. It never is for me. You see, my mind tends to wander a **teeny, weeny** bit sometimes. Okay, who am I kidding? It's more like my mind goes off on **long hiking trips** all by itself and leaves no forwarding address!

Last year at our Year Four Parent-Teacher night Mrs. McGurk told my parents that I had an **"overactive imagination."** Mrs. McGurk didn't really look that **happy** about it.

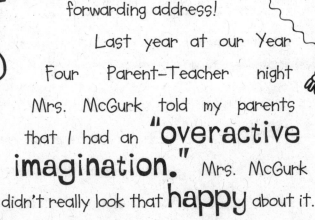

But Mum said, "Rubbish! Imaginations are supposed to be active. The more active the better! Eric's imagination is fine. Perhaps **some** people just need to try a little harder to keep up with it!"

Mrs. McGurk was looking even less happy after Mum said that. My mum was looking pleased. My little sister Katie was looking bored. My dad was looking **embarrassed.** I was looking for a way out of there!

But seriously, how was I supposed to concentrate on what Mr. Winter was going on about when Secret Agent Dale was **handcuffed,** wearing only his

stinky, holey, month-old **underpants**, surrounded by a hundred **deadly** ninjas and about to be shoved off a plank into a pool of crocs, piranha and sea snakes? It just wasn't possible!

I guess that's why even though I **tried** to pay attention, my eyes sort of ended up back on my journal ...

"Move!"

The angry voice came from the angry ninja at his back.

Agent Dale crept forward on the plank. While his toes curled over the edge and gripped tight, his expertly trained secret agent eyes darted back and forth looking for something - anything! - that he could use to save himself. A rusty paper clip perhaps, a tiny piece of broken glass, a lost nose stud, a carelessly misplaced rocket launcher.

But there was nothing. Nothing at all! The situation was hopeless! This time it really looked like the end for ...

"Eric Vale! Have you been listening to anything I've been saying?"

Mr. Winter was standing right beside my desk! How did he get there without me seeing him? Did he **teleport** himself? There was no time to work it out. He was frowning at my journal. I slapped it shut.

"Yes, sir, I've been listening. Every word!"

"Every word? Well, that's excellent, Eric. I'm pleased. So ... what was I just talking about?"

"Talking about? **You,** sir? Just **now?** Well ... **you** ... were talking ... a ... booooooooooouuuuuuuuuuuut ..."

Come on, brain! Help me out here! I really had been concentrating for a little while there. Surely **something** must have got through.

AAAAAOINK! TURN OFF THE POWER! I'M BACON HERE!

Then I had it! Mr. Winter had said something about **Tyrannosaurus rex.** I remembered that because it got me thinking about the movie **Jurassic Park.** Only I thought wouldn't it be funny if it was really called **Jurassic PORK** and all the dinosaurs looked like giant pigs and that made me think about ...

"**Eric?** Any time before nightfall would be good."

"Huh? Oh, right. Um, you were talking about ... um ... **dinosaurs?** Like how they're extinct and everything?"

Mr. Winter pushed out his bottom lip a bit and he nodded.

"Well, yes, Eric. You are completely correct. I **was** talking about dinosaurs ..."

WOOHOO! ALL RIGHTY, THEN! SLAM-DUNKED IT IN ONE! I'VE GOT THE BRAIN OF AN ELEPHANT! I NEVER FORGET! ERIC VALE ROCKS THE CLASSROOM!

"... around twenty minutes ago."

"What's that, sir?"

"I **said,** Eric, that I **was** talking about dinosaur extinction, but that was about twenty minutes ago. Since then, while your mind has obviously been elsewhere, I have been talking about the problems of introduced species

and the alarming number of present-day animals that are on the brink of extinction."

BOO HOO! ALL WRONGY THEN! MY SHOT SAILED CLEAR OVER THE BACKBOARD! I HAVE THE BRAIN OF AN EARTHWORM AND THE MEMORY OF A ... UM ... ER ... YOU KNOW ... THOSE THINGS WITH THE SHORT MEMORY. ERIC VALE SUCKS IN THE CLASSROOM!

SSSSSSSS

"Sorry, Mr. Winter ..."

"I know, Eric. You **always** are. But if I find you tuning out and drifting off into your own little world just **one** more time, then I'm afraid I'll have to confiscate that journal of yours and you will have some catching up to do with me at lunchtime. Now let's see if we can **focus** for the remainder of the lesson, shall we? After all, entire animal species on the brink of extinction is an extremely serious and important topic."

It was too. And the last thing I wanted to do was lose my journal and spend my lunchtime with Mr. Winter! So I did exactly what he asked. I focused. I pushed every other thought out of my head. **Nothing** or **no one** was going to sidetrack me this time. It was definitely time to CONCENTRATE ON THE TOPIC!

All righty then, let's see, animals on the **"brink of extinction."** I was all over it. I had myself right in the "brink of extinction" zone. There was just no room in my mind for anything else but "brink of extinction" stuff. Yep, no doubt about it, being on the "brink of extinction" would totally suck! Wow, just think – what if **you** were the one on the "brink of extinction"? Just **imagine** what that would be like!

I grabbed my pen and threw open my journal.

Looks like I'm on the brink of extinction, just like all those poor, threatened animal species, Agent Dale thought as his toes started to lose their grip.

Nothing could possibly save him now.

But then ... HE SAW IT!

Awesome! Brilliant! Genius!

Except ... I had no idea what Secret Agent Derek "Danger" Dale had just seen that was going to save him! What could it be?

I checked out what Mr. Winter was doing. He was up at the whiteboard **still** going on about something or other, so I looked around the classroom for some ideas.

Let's seeeeeeee ... What could Secret Agent Dale posssssssssssssibly have spotted that he could use in some super-tricky secret agent way to help him escape? Hmmmmmm. What ... could ... it ... beeeeeeee ...? We've got pens ... pencils ... rulers ... staplers ... books ... ribbons ... hair clips. They'd all be **kind** of useful, but no way would you find any of them lying around when you're standing on a plank in just your undies. There had to be **something** else in the classroom that could help me come up with a brilliant idea.

But there was nothing! Nothing at all! The situation was **hopeless!** This time it really looked like the end for my Secret Agent Derek "Danger" Dale story! Nothing could possibly save it now!

But then ... I SAW IT!

Sitting two desks across from me was Big Bob – Class Captain, tug-of-war legend and **small planet.** He was leaning back with his shirt stretched over his stomach. A couple of buttons had popped open. Part of Big Bob's belly was sticking out.

I had my answer! There wasn't a moment to lose. Time to save Derek "Danger" Dale! I began scribbling in my journal ...

The ninja army surrounding Agent Dale was chanting for blood. In seconds he knew his toes would lose their hold on the thin plank and he would plunge to a ghastly death.

But "Danger" Dale wasn't thinking about any of that. He was gazing down at his stomach and the big piece of greasy, grey fluff he'd just plucked from deep within his bellybutton - and he was smiling!

"Could be a bit tricky," Dale said, rubbing the belly-button fluff between two fingers, "but it just might work."

Agent Dale quickly rolled the smelly fluff into a tight pointy shape. He stuck it into the lock of his handcuffs and jiggled it around. The handcuffs clicked open.

YEEEEEEESSSSSSSSSS!

WOOHOOOOOO! Thanks for your help, Big Bob!

But I couldn't stop there, could I? I mean, what about those ninjas? And what about the pool of hungry crocs, flesh—chomping piranha and poisonous sea snakes? What was Derek Dale going to do? He'd need a bomb or some sort of **deadly weapon** to get rid of those things. I scratched my head. I chewed on my pen. If I couldn't think of something, Agent Dale was doomed! But what? He was almost **naked.** Where would he possibly get a deadly weapon from?

Ummmmmmm ... Aaaaaaaahhhhhh ... Maaaaaaaaaaaaybeeeeeeee ... GOT IT! My pen was flying across the page.

Once he was free of the cuffs, Derek whipped off his disgusting, mouldy, month-old undies and threw them into the pool below. As soon as they hit the water it turned green and began to bubble. Dozens of humungous crocodiles struggled to escape but they all collapsed and died. Hundreds of bloated piranha and sea snakes floated belly-up on the surface.

All right! I was **on fire!**

Now for those ninjas!

Derek spun round to face his would-be executioner. He stuck out his hand and pointed the spiky bellybutton fluff at the ninja whose sword had been forcing him to his death. He was the size of a bear and from what Derek could make out, twice as hairy but only half as friendly.

"This is fluff straight from my bellybutton, my friend," Derek shouted as he waved it around, "and I'm not afraid to use it!"

The giant fur-ball ninja frowned and looked down at the puny fluffy spike in Derek's hand. Then he threw back his head and laughed hysterically.

A puny piece of **belly-button fluff?** That's never going to stop a giant ninja with a sword! What was I thinking? Of course that ninja would laugh hysterically. Who wouldn't? What a **dumb** thing for Agent Dale to do. I mean, he must have known he'd just get laughed at ... Hey ... wait on ... Maybe he totally **did** know that ...

This was EXACTLY what Secret Agent Derek Dale was waiting for!

While his opponent was distracted, Derek rolled the bellybutton fluff into a hard pellet and flicked it into the cackling mouth before him. Bear Ninja slammed his jaws shut and clutched at his throat. His eyes bulged. His eyes crossed. His eyes rolled back in his head. He dribbled. His hair fell out. He turned purple. Derek sensed that his opponent was in trouble!

"It's a little known fact," Derek informed him as he began frothing at the mouth like he'd swallowed a bucket of washing powder, "that bellybutton fluff, well past its use-by date, contains twenty-two of the deadliest toxins known to man - or woman (Dale was always politically correct). It should never, I repeat never, be taken internally."

Go Secret Agent Dale!
I was **on a roll!** I was writing like crazy now.

"Thanks-for-the-tip. Must-remember-that," Bear Ninja choked out before he tumbled off the plank, completed a triple somersault and bellyflopped awesomely into the water below. A giant tidal wave of undies-contaminated water splashed from the pool in all directions. It completely soaked the hundred killer ninjas who were standing around it and they all immediately passed out or fell into a coma. The lucky ones didn't survive.

"Another little known fact," Derek said, even though there was no one left to hear him (or see him - which was just as well), "is that my smelly undies, well past their use-by date, contain twenty-THREE of the deadliest toxins known to man - or woman."

It was all just another day at the office for Secret Agent ...

"ERIC VALE!"

Huh? What? My name was being called!

Oh, no! I'd lost concentration and drifted off AGAIN! I was **doomed** to spend lunchtime with Mr. Winter! That was worse than a gobful of Agent Dale's **toxic** bellybutton fluff! Somehow I had to convince Mr. Winter that I'd been listening all along. Before I could stop myself I did a Chewy and jumped up from my seat without thinking.

"Yes, sir! I'm with you! I'm here! I'm paying **attention!** Yep, brink of extinction. I agree totally. **Terrible,** just terrible!"

Then everything went **really quiet.** I looked around the room. The whole class was **staring** at me with these giant frowns like someone had gone around the room and **scrunched up** all their faces. Mr. Winter's regular frown had a frown all of its own. He hadn't called out my name at all.

Chewy told me afterwards what **really** happened.

Apparently Mr. Winter had been talking about how back in the past they brought all these **cane toads** to Australia from Brazil to eat the cane beetles that were **wrecking** the sugar cane crops. Only problem was, when they got

here the cane toads, instead of eating those beetles like they were supposed to, just bred like crazy and started destroying all the native wildlife instead.

When Mr. Winter finished that story he said, "The introduction of cane toads into this country is a very good example of what you people today might call an ... EPIC FAIL!"

Except that's not what I heard.

Chewy said Mr. Winter was looking pretty pleased with himself for coming up with that "epic fail" thing. Or at least he was until I jumped up and blurted out, "Yes, sir! I'm with you! I'm here! I'm paying **attention!** Yep, brink of extinction. I agree totally. **Terrible,** just terrible!"

Then Mr. Winter just looked the same as everyone else in the class - **gobsmacked.**

"Eric Vale, whatever is the matter with you?"

"Aaaaaaaah, nothing, sir. Just thought I ... ummmmm ... heard something. But obviously ... not. My bad!"

I sat right back down as fast as I could. I **almost** got away with it too, but then Martin Fassbender looked at me and then back at Mr. Winter and then back at me, and the frown on his face began slowly disappearing. It was being replaced by a **terrifying grin.**

Next he pointed a finger at me and began making a strange noise.

It sounded like a cat coughing up a fur ball the size of Tasmania. "Aaah...aha...aha...aha...awwwwwwww, I get it. Eric Vale ..." he said as his grin blew up even bigger and freakier.

"... Sounds like ... Epic Fail."

Then Martin turned to the kids around him.

"Don't you get it? Eric Vale – Epic Fail. Ahahahahahah!"

Meredith Murdoch and Bobby Quan got it first. And then it started to spread like it was contagious. All around the room kids with big grins were turning to kids with big frowns and saying, "Eric Vale – Epic Fail. See? Hahahahahahahaha!"

It was like I was one of those YouTube clips and I was going **mega-viral!**

HA HA HA HA HA HA

HA

HA

"Eric Vale, Epic Fail! Get it? Hahahahahahahaha!"

"What's so funny?"

"Eric Vale – Epic Fail. It rhymes!"

"Oh yeah. Hahahahahahahaha!"

"Huh? What's the big joke?"

"Eric Vale, Epic Fail! They're almost the same!"

"Hey, yeah! That's hilarious! Hahahahahahahaha!"

"What's the matter with Eric Vale?"

"He's an EPIC FAIL!"

"I'll say! HAHAHAHAHAHAHAHAHA!"

It just kept growing and growing and getting louder and louder and even Mr. Winter couldn't stop it. Soon everyone in the class was either laughing out loud or grinning like a monkey.

HA HA HA HA HA HA

HA HA AH HA HA

Everyone except me.

And that's how I got the stupid nickname **"Epic Fail."** I wasn't that worried about it at first. I figured if I ignored it and didn't do anything else stupid for a while, it would just go away. At least that was my plan.

That turned out to be a bit of an epic fail as well.

HA HA HA HA

o•o•o•o•o•o•o•o•o•o•o•o•

The next morning at school, it started.

For example:

I'm practising my pen twirling while Mr. Winter is reading out morning notices and it spins from my fingers and bounces off my desk on to the floor.

HA HA HA HA

I hear a voice from behind me.

"Eric Vale - Epic Fail!"

It's Martin Fassbender. Typical.

Then I get **one** word wrong on our weekly thirty-word spelling test.

"Eric Vale - Epic Fail!"

Fassbender again. Meanwhile he's got **sixteen** words wrong AND he's spelt Fassbender with three esses at the top of his page!

Martin
Fassssbender

liberry
vakyume
conshus
exeptibble
hirarky
weerd
dissaplin
restaront
misschivus
skejool

Later on at morning tea I buy a fruit juice popper. I try to stick the plastic straw in the little hole in the top. But I'm squeezing the cardboard container too hard and when the straw goes through, the juice shoots straight up one of my nostrils and dribbles out the other.

"Epic Eric - Fail Vale!"

It's Martin's best buddy, Tyrone Knowles. Tyrone makes Martin look like a **genius.** I'm pretty sure that Tyrone could make a bowl of **porridge** look reasonably **bright.**

Back in class Mr. Winter calls me out the front to write an answer to a maths problem on the board.

On the way I **almost,** but don't actually, trip over someone's foot. A voice whispers —

"Eric Vale – Epic Fail!"

It's not Martin or Tyrone this time. It's Meredith Murdoch. And some kids around her are smiling and giggling.

I write the answer on the board. I actually get it right. YAY ME! Meredith looks disappointed. I go back to my seat. I feel lots of eyes on me now. They're all watching me. They're all waiting. And I know why. They want me to muck something up so **they** can get a chance to say, "Eric Vale – Epic Fail!" too.

This was bad. This was really bad. My new stupid nickname was catching on. It was beginning to stick! It was like **superglue.** I had to get it off me fast, otherwise I was in **big trouble.**

For the rest of the morning I turned into a **statue.** I did nothing and said nothing in case I made a mistake. I didn't dare work on **The Totally Awesome Action Adventures of Secret Agent Derek "Danger" Dale.** All my attention was on Mr. Winter and on not doing anything **dumb.** But I was starting to feel the **pressure.** I could feel my mind getting its hiking gear on. I knew I was about to crack!

ERIC VALE

Then the **new girl** arrived and saved me. Or at least that's what I thought.

o•o•o•o•o•o•o•o•o•o•o•o•o•

The new girl's name was Aasha Alsufi. Mr. Winter told us last term she was joining our class, but I'd forgotten all about it until she turned up at the door with Principal Porter.

The new girl was from somewhere called Somalia. That's in Africa. Mr. Winter wrote the name on the board and we searched it on the internet so we'd know something about it before she arrived. They have **wars** in Somalia. Heaps of wars. And **droughts**. And these big camps filled with people. Heaps of them too.

Somalia →

Mr. Winter said the new girl had been through a lot, but he wouldn't say what exactly. He just told us that when she arrived she would be very **nervous** about being in a new place and he was really counting on us to be **friendly** and to make her feel safe and welcome.

The new girl was wearing a red scarf-type thing that went right over her head like a hoodie and then wrapped around her face. Her skin was dark brown. Her head was bent way down and she **stared** at the floor the whole time. She had a copy of our school diary in her hands. She looked like she was trying to **strangle** it to death.

Mr. Winter introduced her to our class and said the usual welcoming-type stuff, but the new girl didn't look up once. Then Mr. Winter took her to a desk right up the front in between Li Wan and Sophie Peters, who are the two nicest girls in our class by about a million light years. Well, **probably.** I mean I haven't really thought about it **that** much.

For the rest of the morning Aasha Alsufi kept her head down so low you couldn't even see her face, and she stared at her school diary like she was Gollum and it was **the One Ring.**

NICENESS (m.l.y)

Li & Sophie

Rest of class

When lunchtime came, lots of people really did try to make her feel welcome just like Mr. Winter asked.

Li and Sophie smiled and talked to her a lot and asked her if she wanted to come and sit with them out in the playground.

But the new girl just shook her head and looked **worried.**

Then Big Bob came over because he's the class captain. But the new girl just stared at Big Bob, who was about four times her size and looked even **more worried.**

Then Meredith Murdoch and a whole bunch of her friends sort of elbowed their way past Li and Sophie and Big Bob (not easy) and started asking the new girl all about Somalia and who her favourite pop star was and what her favourite movie and TV shows were and did she have a pet lion and what did she do on the weekend and stuff like that.

And the new girl went from worried to **confused.**

Then Micky Micareeno and Chewy fought their way through the crowd, bouncing a soccer ball and waving a bat around and asking her if she wanted to play football or cricket with them.

And the new girl passed confused and went straight to **scared.**

Then Martin Fassbender, Tyrone Knowles, Vinnie Romano and Pete Bunter jumped in and did their best to make her laugh by showing off their favourite tricks – ones like **cracking their knuckles** really loudly, arm wrestling, throwing lollies in the air and catching them (sometimes) in their mouths, seeing who could touch their nose with their tongue, turning their eyelids **inside out** and playing tunes using different parts of their bodies.

And the new girl **ran** outside.

WARP!

After lunch the seat between Li Wan and Sophie Peters was empty. I thought we would get into a **heap of trouble** for scaring the new girl off. But we didn't.

Mr. Winter just thanked us all for trying to do the right thing. He said that **maybe** we tried a bit **too** hard and that the new girl Aasha Alsufi needed "a little more time and space to settle in and find her feet."

The good news was that we hadn't **frightened her off** for good and that she was coming back to school the next day.

AASHA'S FEET

I was really glad she was coming back. She seemed nice. The other thing I was pretty pleased about was that in the **excitement** over Aasha Alsufi's arrival, no one was interested in me any more. Everyone was just focused on her. It looked like they'd all **forgotten** about the Eric Vale – Epic Fail thing completely.

And they probably would have, if it hadn't been for the school assembly **disaster.**

After that, it was like I'd written Eric Vale – Epic Fail in their brains with one of those thick marker pens. A **permanent** ink one.

HEY! THAT'S MY BRAIN!

ERIC VALE EPIC FAIL

Epic Fail No. 2:
The School Assembly

Aasha Alsufi did come back the next day, and even though everyone gave her **space** like Mr. Winter said, there was still this **huge contest** going on to see who could be the first to get her to talk or smile. **Epic fails all round.**

Aasha Alsufi just either nodded or shook her head and seemed much happier when she was left alone.

THE GYM

But for me, things were looking up. I went through most of the week without hearing the words "Eric Vale – Epic Fail" once.

Then came Friday – school assembly day.

This assembly was **special**, because this was the week our class was **in charge** of running it. That meant Mr. Winter had to pick people for different jobs like MC-ing, reading the notices and introducing the speakers. And we had to provide the **entertainment.** That's where Chewy and I came in.

We were given the job of acting out a scene from this story we'd been reading in class. That meant we had to memorise our lines and dress up and everything. Chewy and I were supposed to play identical twins.

PSSST. YOU'RE FACING THE WRONG WAY.

Chewy reckoned it didn't really make sense because our eyes were **totally different** colours.

Probably the only reason we got chosen was because Chewy **volunteered** us. Chewy volunteers for everything. He doesn't care what it is. As soon as he heard Mr. Winter say, "Now I need two boys to volunteer to ..." Chewy stuck up his hand and **blurted out,** "Me and Eric'll do it!"

For a minute there Mr. Winter **went a bit pale.** So did I when I heard what we had to do.

PICK US

I wanted to **quit** straightaway but Chewy talked me out of it.

"If you think you **can't,** you **won't,** Eric," he told me. "But if you think you **can,** you **will!"** Chewy was **positive!** that we'd do great. I had my doubts, but I agreed because I knew Chewy would **bug me to death** if I didn't.

So Mr. Winter said, "Right. Good. Yes, that's ... **excellent.** Looks like we've got the boys' roles all sorted out. Now we just need someone for the girl's part. How about you, Li?"

That's Li Wan. She's the smartest person in our class (although I'm pretty sure Chewy thinks **he** is). Anyway, Li said yes and Mr. Winter didn't look quite so pale after that. The **best** thing about doing the acting was that we got to dress up in costumes, with **swords** and everything, on account of the scene was set in the time of **knights** and **castles**. Li was like a **princess** or a lady or something. And we all had to wear these special little microphones on our collars so we could move around the stage and everyone could hear us, which was **pretty cool.**

On the day, all the school, including the Year Sixes and Sevens, got together in the assembly hall. I was pretty nervous because this was just the sort of place where a really bad Eric Vale - Epic Fail **disaster** could take place. But even though Chewy decided to add a few of his own made-up lines during the performance to "improve" it, the whole thing went really well. At the end, the three of us got a big round of **applause.**

After our act was finished we had to sit up on stage for the rest of the assembly. As we headed for our seats Li reminded me to turn off my lapel mic. I flicked the switch and watched the little green light **disappear.**

Then I made sure I reminded Chewy to turn his off as well.

All the Year Fives who had done assembly stuff were sitting in a row of chairs on one side of the stage. On the other side were the seats for the Principal, the Deputy Principal, Mr. Winter and our **special** guest speaker.

Our special guest speaker was Mrs. Doreen Dorrington. She was the Deputy Lord Mayor. She was telling us all about herself and how she went to Moreton Hill Primary School about **a million years ago** when she was a little girl, and she went on ... and on ... and on ... and on ... **and on.**

And just when you thought she had to be finished ... she went on ... and on ... **and on** **... some more!**

I was trying my best to pay attention to the Deputy Mayor's talk because Mr. Winter had given us a huge speech about "being on show" while we were up on stage and about "setting an example" and about not **"fidgeting** around and **distracting** everyone" in the assembly hall. I promised myself that this was going to be one time I wouldn't let my mind drift off. No **unauthorised hiking trips!**

But it was tough. Really tough. Mrs. Dorrington's talk was like **torture.** That's all I could think about while I was sitting up there on stage trying not to fidget. Man, this is **torture!** This talk is exactly like **torture.** If you really wanted to **torture** someone, you know what you could do ...

Torture was no stranger to Secret Agent Derek "Danger" Dale. He sat tied up in a chair. In front of him stood the most evil of all his evil enemies, the incredibly evil Doctor Evil MacEvilness.

He really wasn't a nice guy.

"So, Secret Agent Derek 'Danger' Dale, we meet at last!"

"No, actually we've met lots of times before," said Dale with a frown. "Remember how you keep trying to kill me and take over the world but I keep stopping you EVERY SINGLE TIME?"

"Of course! That is SO annoying! I thought your face looked familiar. So tell me, Dale, are you going to give me the Secret Code or not?"

"I can't."

"Why not?"

"Because if I tell you then it wouldn't be a secret any more, would it?"

"Perhaps your tongue will loosen if I pull this switch and send one hundred thousand volts of electricity racing through your body?"

"I doubt it. Fortunately I've been trained to take up to one hundred thousand ... and one volts."

"Yes, but what if at the same time I have my evil sidekicks tickle you under the feet and arms with ostrich feathers, pull out your nose hairs with tweezers and drag your fingernails across this specially prepared blackboard?"

"You swine! Now I know why they call you evil Doctor Evil MacEvilness. It's because ... you're MEAN!"

MacEvilness tossed back his head and cackled like a maniac.

"Maybe so, Dale, but you have to admit, I have a terrific sense of humour! Now give me the Secret Code!"

"Never! There's nothing you can do to make me give up the Code. NOTHING!"

"Nothing?" MacEvilness said with a sickly grin. "Not even THIS?"

The incredibly evil Doctor pulled a cord and a curtain opened behind him. Secret Agent Derek "Danger" Dale gasped in horror. His face turned white with fear.

"YOU WOULDN'T! YOU COULDN'T! NOT EVEN YOU, MACEVILNESS, WOULD STOOP THAT LOW!"

"Just watch me, Agent Dale. When you're ready, MRS. DORRINGTON. Take ALL the time you need."

Deputy Mayor Doreen Dorrington stepped forward and started to speak into the microphone.

"Well, when I was a little girl, things were very different from what they are today. Can you believe, when I was a little girl we didn't even have a television set? When I was a little girl there were no computers either. When I was a little girl, my only toys were a piece of string, half a bent paper clip and a dead cockroach. For dinner we had a slice of stale bread to share between nine of us and on special occasions, a bowl of steam. Why, when I was a little girl ..."

Secret Agent Derek "Danger" Dale clamped his hands over his ears and screamed.

WAAAAAAAAAAHH!!!!!!!!!!!

The feedback from a microphone echoed around the hall. Suddenly I remembered where I was! I looked across the stage. Mrs. Dorrington was **still** talking! I couldn't take it any more. I leant down to Chewy and whispered out the side of my mouth.

WHAT TIME DOES THIS FINISH?

"I think they should call her Mrs. **BORING**-ton, not Dorrington. 'Hi, I'm Deputy Mayor BORE-een BORING-ton. **I-BORE-DEAD-PEOPLE!'"**

Chewy twisted up his mouth so he wouldn't laugh. And then something strange happened. All of a sudden everyone in the assembly hall started talking and laughing right in the middle of Mrs. Dorrington's speech. Talk about **rude!** Someone was going to be in **BIG** trouble!

I looked over at Principal Porter and our Deputy Ms. Carter and Mr. Winter. They all seemed **pretty upset.**

→ 73 ←

They were looking around trying to work out what caused all the noise and making **angry bulldog faces** at everyone in the hall to get them to be quiet.

I leant down and spoke out the side of my mouth to Chewy again.

"What just happened? Did Mrs. **BORING**-ton **BORE** someone to death or something?"

Suddenly everyone in the hall starts **killing themselves laughing** again. What was the **matter** with these people? Didn't they have any manners?

HA
HA
HA HA
HA HA

I leant across again.

"Hey, what's the bet that when Mrs. **BORING**–ton was at school she was a **BORE**–der."

More laughing.

"What's going on, Chewy?" I whispered. "Hey, check out Mr. Winter. His hair's red enough already. If his face goes any redder I reckon he'll **explode** like a tomato!"

Now everyone's **really cracking up!** And they're doing something else as well. They're all looking in my direction. Some of them are pointing. I look behind me to see what they're laughing at but there's nothing there. **Weird.** I turn back.

I look around the assembly hall. They're laughing even harder now. The only person I can see who's **not laughing** is Aasha, the new girl. She just looks a bit frightened and confused by all the noise.

Then I see Martin. He's slapping Tyrone on the back with one hand and **pointing at me** with the other. His mouth is making word shapes, and the word shapes it's making are ...

EPIC FAIL!

I turn to Chewy.

"Chewy, I think everyone's gone **totally** nu–"

And that's when I see the microphone on his collar. How can I miss it? It's right next to my mouth.

AND THE GREEN LIGHT IS ON!

Everyone has heard every single word I've said! I look back to the Deputy Mayor. She's giving me an **evil stare** that even evil Doctor Evil MacEvilness would be jealous of. I swing back to Chewy.

"I told you to turn your mic **off!**"

"Off?" Chewy said, scratching his head. "It **was** off. I thought you said to turn it **on.**"

"What? Why would I ..."

Then I realised **everyone's laughing even louder** because everything we're saying now is still **bouncing** around the hall! I go to grab Chewy's mic, but before I can, Mr. Winter grabs both of us by the shirts and pulls us off the stage. Mr. Winter's stronger than I thought.

My feet are hardly touching the ground. We get a big round of **applause.** Bigger than for our acting. Chewy even manages to throw in a couple of bows as we get **dragged** away.

When we're well and truly offstage and hidden behind the side curtains, Mr. Winter jabs his finger at our mics. He doesn't look happy. In fact he's doing a great impression of a **serial killer.** It looks like his red hair has run and stained his face. He speaks in a **scary whisper** with his teeth closed.

"Are. Those. Things. OFF?"

I check mine. Chewy checks his.

"Off," we say together.

Then I expect Mr. Winter to really go **bananas.** But he doesn't. He just stands there for a long time with his eyes closed, shaking his head. So I thought I'd better say something to break the silence.

"Sorry, sir. I didn't mean it. Honest. But ... she was a bit ... you know ..."

Mr. Winter snapped his eyes open and stared down at us. He was back in **serial killer mode**. Chewy and I took a step away.

"**Boring?** Is that what you were going to say, Eric? That Mrs. Dorrington is a bit **boring?** Well, of **course** she's **boring!** I know she's **boring!** You know she's **boring!** Everybody knows she's **boring**. She's the Deputy Mayor of Boring! She probably invented **boring!**

HEY...

It wouldn't surprise me if she had a Masters
Degree in Boring from Boring University!
If she was any more **boring**
she'd be a weapon of mass
destruction! Doctors could use
her as a general anaesthetic!
Engineers could use her to
bore tunnels! But just
because you know someone's
boring doesn't mean you
have to say ..."

Mr. Winter **froze.**

He turned his head slowly. He
was listening to something. I could hear
it too. It was coming from the assembly
hall. It was like there was a **riot** going on
out there. And there was laughing too. **Lots**
and **lots** of it. Mr. Winter looked at my mic.

So did I. Then we both looked at Chewy's.

So did Chewy. He unpinned it from his collar and held it up. There was a light **glowing** on the side of it. He **frowned.**

"Green means OFF, doesn't it?" he asked.

I grabbed the mic from Chewy's hand and clicked the switch. The green light disappeared. Mr. Winter just stood there for a couple of seconds. Then he leant back on the wall behind him. He knocked his head against it three times **(hard!)** then slid slowly down until he was sitting on the floor with his long legs stretched out in front of him.

Chewy and I looked at each other.

Then at Mr. Winter. And we waited.

And waited. And waited some more.

"**Uuuummmmm** ... would you like us to ... put the mics ... back in the storage cupboard now, Mr. Winter?"

Mr. Winter looked up at us and smiled. He seemed to be taking it pretty well considering the whole school including the Principal had just heard him **raving on** about the Deputy Mayor.

"Would you, Eric? That would be ... **lovely.**"

I was thinking maybe Mr. Winter had hit his head a bit **too** hard against the wall. When we came back from the storage cupboard he was still sitting on the floor – sort of hugging his legs. He was still smiling. **At nothing.**

"Aaaaaaaah, anything **else** we can do for you, sir?"

Mr. Winter smiled some more and bobbed his head slowly up and down.

"Why yes, as a matter of fact, Eric, there is. Before you leave, would you mind ... just shooting me?"

o•o•o•o•o•o•o•o•o•o•o•

Moreton Hill Primary School Newsletter No 11

View from the Principal's Desk!

Last Friday we were **delighted** and **honoured** to have Deputy Mayor and ex-student Doreen Dorrington address our school assembly. What a **treat** for the children! Deputy Mayor Dorrington is a past student of Moreton Hill Primary School and she gave a **fascinating** and **informative** insight into what life and school were like when she was a little girl.

Many times during her speech the assembly hall was filled with much **laughter.** Our sincere thanks to Doreen for her highly **amusing** and educational talk and for her Council's continuing generous support of our building fund. I know I speak for everyone at Moreton Hill Primary School when I say we can't wait for Deputy Mayor Dorrington to return and tell us more about her **enthralling** and **highly entertaining** life.

A special mention too goes to Mr. Brian Winter's Year Five class for running such a well-organised, entertaining and, at times, **surprising** assembly. In related news, Mr. Winter has kindly **volunteered** to be in charge of organising this year's school fete. This is a **very big undertaking** and I am especially grateful to Mr. Winter for so **generously** offering his services.

Peter Porter

I think Principal Porter should get a job teaching creative writing. He's **a natural!** I was wishing that I could just rewrite the whole school assembly **disaster** and make it turn out the way I wanted.

When we got back to the classroom there was something I did have to write, thanks to Mr. Winter: an essay on **The Importance of Being Polite at All Times.** Chewy asked if Mr. Winter was going to have to write something like that for Principal Porter. **Bad move.** Chewy got an essay on **The Importance of Knowing the Difference Between an OFF and ON Switch.**

But writing the essay didn't worry me that much. What really worried me was that my "Epic Fail" nickname was back, and not only that, it was up **in big flashing lights** for the whole school to see. And I'd put it there!

OFF
ON

ERIC VALE EPIC FAIL EVERY NIGHT ONLY!!!!

Martin even came up with a new term for when something went wrong. He named it after me. He called it an **Eric Fail**. A few other kids started to use it too. I was becoming **famous.** For all the **wrong** reasons. I had to DO SOMETHING!

o•o•o•o•o•o•o•o•o•o•

FAMOUS!
(BUT IN A BAD WAY)

JUST DRIVIN' ME NUTS...

On Saturday morning I went over to Chewy's house. He lives in the next street. We were in his room checking out his new computer game.

"Chewy, this Eric Vale – Epic Fail thing is **driving me nuts!** You gotta help me do something about it!"

Beside me William Choo-Choo Rodriguez bit his lip and squinted his eyes.

He nodded his head thoughtfully. He didn't say anything for ages. He looked like he might be coming up with **a really great plan.** Then he spoke.

"Do something about **what?**"

"About the Eric Vale – Epic Fail thing, of course! What else would I be talking about?"

Chewy nodded his head thoughtfully again.

"Riiiiight. Uhuh. Yeah, I see. Of course," he said before screwing up his face. "But **why?**"

"WHY? **WHY!** BECAUSE I DON'T WANT THE STUPID NICKNAME EPIC FAIL, THAT'S WHY!"

"Really? I think it's kind of **cool.**"

"Yes of **course** you do. But you think Choo–Choo's cool, don't you? You'd probably think Booger Brain was cool!"

COOL!

"Hey," Chewy said, raising his eyebrows, **"Booger Brain** – not bad!"

"Not bad!"

"Yeah, like it **could** mean you've got this **enormous** brain or something."

"Right. And I suppose it's **green** and **hanging out** of your nose, is it?"

I was starting to wonder if it was a **smart idea** coming to Chewy for help. The problem with Chewy was, he never saw anything as a problem and no matter what anyone else said, he always thought he was right.

It was like that day with the crossword when he got his nickname. He still reckoned "Choo-Choo" was the correct answer even when Meredith Murdoch (who else?) pointed out to him at lunchtime that not only was his answer "wrong" but it was also "dumb," since it didn't even have the right number of letters in it to begin with.

Of course anyone else would have just kept quiet and taken it. You know, give up while you're waaaaaaaaaaaay behind. But not Chewy. Ooooooh no. That's because in Chewy's mind he's never wrong. So naturally he just had to argue.

"It does so have the right number of letters. As long as you spell it 'C-H-U-C-H-U.'"

Which almost causes Meredith to have a **heart attack.**

"What? The answer's a **seven**-letter word. Before, your stupid answer had too **many** letters. Now it hasn't got **enough** letters!"

"Then spell it 'C–H–U–C–H–O–O.'"

Near heart attack number two for Meredith.

"What! That's **insane!** You can't change the spelling to whatever you like just to make it fit! None of your other answers will work now."

"Yes they will."

"Okay then, what did you put for two down? The clue is **What cars travel on.** The answer **has** to be 'road' because it starts with the 'r' from the second letter of 'freight.'

But you've got an 'h' there from your **stupid** and **wrong** 'Chu-Choo.' See, I told you. It doesn't work!"

"Does too," William said, "'cause the answer's not 'road,' it's 'highway.'"

Call the ambulance – Meredith is having a fit.

"What! Are you crazy? That's even **stupider!** That's the **stupidest** thing I've ever heard! It has to be a **four**-letter word. No way will 'highway' work."

"It will if you spell it 'H-W-A-Y,'" William informed her.

Too late. Call the undertaker.

Back in Chewy's room I decided to give it one more try.

MEREDITH MURDOCH

'TWAS FREIGHT THAT TOOK HER

"Come on, Chewy. I need your help here. How can I get people to stop calling me Eric Vale – Epic Fail?"

Chewy looked all thoughtful once more. I wasn't holding out much hope this time round.

"Gee, I don't know, Eric. Maybe if you wanna stop the epic fail thing, you gotta do something to make people forget it. You know, maybe have some kind of ... epic win."

"An epic win? Like what? It's not just a few kids in our class any more. It's spreading around the school now. What could I ever do that would be that epically awesome?"

Chewy went quiet again. Then he snapped his fingers.

"Hey, what about **winning** the School Project Award?"

The School Project Award was presented every year. Anyone from any year could enter a project of their choice under one of four categories: Maths, Science, Arts or Literature. Heaps of smart kids entered it. There were two main prizes. **Project of the Year,** judged by a panel of head teachers including the Principal, and the **People's Choice Award,** voted by students, parents and the other teachers.

"The School Project Award? That's **crazy.** Some **genius** in Year Six or Seven who builds a working **time machine** or comes up with a chemical formula for changing **old toenail clippings** into gold usually wins that."

$$\frac{TC + Ne}{\sqrt{x^2 + \theta}} = \bigtriangleup^{3}$$

$$\int_{0.097}^{x}$$ XYZ

"Remember, Eric, if you think you **can't,** you **won't**. But if you think you **can,** you **will**," Chewy said.

"Really. What if you **know** you can't? What happens then?"

Chewy shook his head. "When you're **negative,** you're just saying **no** to your own **potential,** Eric."

$$\frac{\left(\frac{x - \alpha}{7.1136}\right) \times \sqrt{\cdots}}{42} = Au$$

"Yeah, well, in this case, I'm just saying **no** to my potential failure."

"**Failure** is just ..."

"I know, I know, Chewy – **delayed success!** I have a feeling my success is going to be delayed for the rest of my life."

"Doubt it," Chewy said. "But anyway, maybe you're right. Maybe it's not such a good **idea** going for the School Project Award this year."

That didn't sound like Chewy. He **never** gave in that easily.

"Why not?"

"Because I'm pretty sure I'm going to **win** it this year."

Now **that** was more like it!

"What? You? Have you even got a project?"

"Sure. Right there on my desk."

I went over and stood beside Chewy's desk.

"Where is it? All I can see are R2 and C3."

R2 and C3 were Chewy's guinea pigs. Everyone thinks he named them after those **Star Wars** droids R2D2 and C3PO. Which he sort of did, but their real names are actually R2 **Do Poo** and C3 **Pee On Everything.** You can probably guess why.

"R2 and C3 **are** my project."

"**They're** your project? What do you mean? What category are you entering?"

"That's one of the brilliant things about my entry, Eric. It covers all four categories! Maths, Science, Arts **and** Literature."

"What? How can two guinea pigs in a smelly cage possibly be a Maths, Science, Arts and Literature project?"

"Because I'm doing **other stuff** as well."

This I just **had** to hear.

"Other stuff? Like what?"

"Like calculations."

"What kind of calculations?"

"Complex **mathematical** calculations."

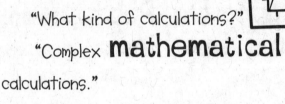

Chewy pulled out a big sheet of cardboard from behind his desk.

"These ones."

The sheet had two graphs on it. One was labelled **R2** and the other **C3**. The bottom of each graph was marked with dates and each vertical axis was marked **Number of pellets**.

"See, I'm recording how much R2 and C3 **poop every day** and I'm plotting it on these graphs. I'm also comparing their rate of poops to each other and to the different kinds of food they eat. Like, I'm working out the average number of **poops per carrot** and the average number of **poops per apple.** It's **very** complicated stuff. I have to take into account all sorts of things like the different sizes and weights of the apples and carrots. Lucky for me, all the poops are almost exactly identical."

I stared at him. I blinked. He was still there. It wasn't **a weird dream.** "But ... why?"

Chewy **shrugged** his shoulders as if the answer was **obvious.**

"For scientific research."

"Right. Of course. Well, that's great, Chewy. I'm **proud** of you. You're helping make the world a better place. But I still don't see how that covers all four categories? You've got Maths and **maybe** some Science, but what about Arts and Literature?

"Well, for the Literature bit I've written an **awesome poem.** Took me ages."

Chewy opened a folder on his desk and handed me a sheet of paper. There was a poem on it, all right. I read it out.

GUINEA PIGS

G reat pets!

U rinate everywhere!

I n a cage is where they live!

N eed to have their toenails clipped!

E at lettuce, carrots, celery and apples!

A nd other stuff!

P oop lots and lots!

I ntelligent – not very!

G iant front teeth for chewing!

S queal when hungry – or squeezed!

by William C. C. Rodriguez

"Did you notice how it's a poem **about** guinea pigs and at the same time, the first letters of all the lines together actually **spell** the word guinea pigs? I did that on purpose," Chewy said proudly.

"**Wow,**" I said, "now that you mention it ..."

I was almost too **scared** to push the next question out of my mouth.

"And so ... for the **Arts** category, then?"

"That's the **killer,** Eric. That's where I totally blow the judges away. That's what gives me ... **the edge.**"

I waited as Chewy's round face split into a big smile.

"I'm **recycling** R2 and C3's poop pellets and making them into a **picture!**"

"You're wha ..."

Before I could finish my question Chewy had whipped out another cardboard sheet from behind his desk – a giant one this time. He was holding it inches away from my face. It had a **strange smell** about it.

"Pretty awesome, hey?"

I leant back a little to take it all in – and to get my breath back before I passed out. It was an almost completed, life-sized picture of a person made entirely out of **thousands** of guinea pig droppings glued to cardboard. Something about the way the ears stuck out, the cheesy grin, the little round head and the spiky hair seemed familiar.

"Is ... that ... supposed to be ... a self-portrait?"

"Sure is," Chewy said, looking super-pleased, "except I like to call it ... a self-**poo**trait!"

There are times when I think that maybe my good friend William Choo-Choo Rodriguez might be from another planet. All the other times I'm **sure** he is.

"Well, Chewy, you've obviously got the School Project Award all tied up, so what about me? What am I gonna do to beat this Eric Vale – Epic Fail thing? What other sort of epic win could I have?"

"You got me," Chewy said as he grabbed some fresh pellets from R2 and C3's cage and began gluing them to the sheet.

PLANET CHEWRANUS

W.C.C.R

"Maybe you need to go to someone else for help."

"But who?"

We both thought about that for around a **micro-second.**

"Big Bob," we said at exactly the same time.

o•o•o•o•o•o•o•o•o•o•o•o•o•

Of course Big Bob could help! Big Bob always helped! That's what Big Bob did. He was the friendliest, most helpful guy in the world. Even teachers went to Big Bob for help. That's why he was class captain and the **most popular guy** in Year Five and almost the whole school.

Big Bob helped move heavy stuff.

Big Bob helped kids with their homework.
Big Bob helped new kids settle in (except
for Aasha Alsufi, but we were all bombing
out there). Big Bob helped organise
class activities. Big Bob helped keep
Martin and Tyrone under control.
Big Bob was an **expert** helper!

"I don't think I can help,"
Big Bob said.

It was before school on
Monday morning. Chewy and
I were sitting with Robert
"Big Bob" Falou on one of
the lunch benches.

"There must be **some-
thing** you can do?"
Big Bob narrowed
his eyes.

P.H.D
Helping

Big Bob

"Well, you said Martin and Tyrone are the main ones carrying on about the Eric Vale – Epic Fail thing, right? So maybe you just have to stop them. I suppose I could give them a 'friendly' **head squeeze** if you want."

Big Bob was famous for his head squeezes. He did it to everyone. Except the girls, of course. The head squeeze was kind of like Big Bob's hug. He'd just wrap one of his big arms around your head and squeeze it a bit. It **didn't hurt** at all, and getting a head squeeze from Big Bob was the same as getting a pat on the back or a handshake from anyone else. It was his way of saying he liked you.

A Big Bob head squeeze

was definitely a good thing.

Unless he gave you a "friendly" head squeeze, which looked exactly the same as a normal head squeeze only it was actually a bit **less** "friendly" and a bit **more** "squeeze." Not that Big Bob would ever hurt anyone. It's just sometimes he had to kind of remind **some** people that he could. Martin and Tyrone mainly. Mostly for being **rude** to the girls. Big Bob didn't like that much.

I have to admit that getting Big Bob to put the squeeze on Martin and Tyrone

No!
NOT THE FRIENDLY!

was **very tempting** – even if it didn't work. But my **problem** was bigger than just the two of them. I had to show a whole lot of other people that I wasn't the epic fail that it looked like I was turning into.

INSERT EPIC WIN HERE

"Nah, thanks anyway, Big Bob. I think Chewy's right. It needs to be something I do. I need **a proper epic** win to change people's minds. Something **like** the School Project Award, except it has to be something I've at least got **one chance** in a **million** of actually doing."

We all went quiet for quite a long time then. I thought I might have set Big Bob an **impossible** task. But Big Bob never liked to let anyone down.

TICK
TICK
TICK

I could see his mind ticking over. After a while he began to nod his head slowly.

"The swimming carnival," he said. "It's next Monday."

"Yeah. What about it?"

"Well, what's the **only** thing that Martin is any good at?"

That was **easy.**

"Swimming."

"And what does he **always** win without hardly trying?"

Also easy.

"The first division freestyle final at the swimming carnival."

"So that's it. That's how you have your epic win. Beat Martin in the first division freestyle final. He just thinks he's **always** going to win. But you're a pretty good swimmer.

MARLIN FISHBENDER

1st

You always make the first division. Just think. If you beat Martin, then how can he call **you** an epic fail? What would that make **him?** And if you stop Martin, you stop Tyrone. Plus you'll have your **big win** in front of the whole school, and I bet a lot of people would love to see Martin get beaten. You'll be **a legend.** Yeah. I reckon that's it. You beat Martin at the swimming carnival next Monday, I don't think **anyone** will be calling you an epic fail after that."

Everything Big Bob said was absolutely true! It was a brilliant plan! Perfect! Except for that bit about me beating the **best** swimmer in Year Five, a swimmer I'd never even got close to in the past, a swimmer who **trained,** who was in a proper **squad,** a swimmer who could actually dream of going to the **OLYMPICS** one day without people locking him up in a padded cell. **And** I had to do all that in front of the entire school in only one week's time.

Yes, that'll happen. Remember, if you think you can't, you won't! If you think you can, **YOU'RE MAD!**

LET ME OUT! I GOTTA GET TO THE OLYMPICS!

"You can do it, Eric," Chewy said, clenching his fist. "You really can. I believe in you, man!"

Which was nice, except William Choo-Choo Rodriguez also believed that it was possible to win the School Project Award with a self-**poo**trait. But I was getting desperate now and Big Bob's plan was the only plan I had. So I had to make myself believe that it was possible too.

Time for **positive thinking** for **positive results!**

"Okay. I think it's crazy but I'll give it a shot!" I said, and stood up to leave.

"Hey, Eric, look." Chewy laughed with a snort. "You've got a big bit of gum stuck to your pants!"

I looked behind me. There was a long sticky grey line stretching from the back of my school shorts to the bench.

"Hahahahahaha! Eric Vale – Epic Fa–" Chewy **froze** with his mouth open. "Oh ... yeah ... right ... Sorry, Eric ... I forgot. You don't like that much, do you?"

This was going to be harder than I thought.

Epic Fails
Nos 3 to 7

One thing for sure. I had **no chance** of beating Martin without help. So straightaway I joined the after-school swimming sessions that Mr. Heatherington, our PE teacher, was running for anyone who wanted to prepare for the carnival.

   Martin didn't show up, of course. He thought he didn't have to practise to **thrash** the rest of us. And he was right. Besides, he had his **real** swimming club **outside of school** to train with.

My **only hope** was that he wasn't anywhere near in full training mode yet. To have any chance at all, I knew I had to catch him off guard. It's not that I'm a bad swimmer, I guess. It's just that I've never thought much about it before. Just jump in and go like crazy is my method. But Mr. Heatherington showed me what I was doing wrong with my strokes and how I could kick slower but smarter and still go faster! After a few sessions, I was swimming better than ever before!

Meanwhile, my plan in class that week was to keep my head down and not draw any more attention to myself. I didn't want any more ERIC VALE – EPIC FAILS thrown at me. But it seemed that the more I tried to do everything **right**, the more everything went **wrong!**

Here are the week's highlights of what Mr. and Mrs. Rodriguez would call my **epic delayed successes!**

MONDAY: At lunchtime I'm in the queue at the tuckshop and I'm waiting for the little Year Two kid in front of me to finish with the tomato sauce bottle. He's **squeezing** and **thumping** it and hardly anything's coming out. The tuckshop mum says, "You'll have to put a bit **more muscle** in, sweetie. That one's about done."

Then I notice Aasha Alsufi sitting by herself under a tree and I smile at her but she just **stares** at me with her big brown eyes then goes back to scribbling in her diary.

Oh well, no one else had been able to get a smile or a word out of her either. When I turn back the Year Two kid is finished. Finally! So I grab the sauce bottle, aim it at my meat pie and give it the **Iron Man's Mother of all squeezes.**

And tomato sauce spurts out of it like it's **exploding** from a high pressure fire hose! While I was looking at Aasha and trying to get her to smile, the tuckshop mum must have changed the old bottle for a full one. Three rows of kids at the tuckshop are spattered with sauce. It looks like a **massacre!**

Miss Cahill is on playground duty. She glances over.

She starts shrieking, "Get the first aid kit! Call an ambulance! **Don't panic,** anyone! Evacuate the school! Run for your lives!" Everyone else is **screaming** or shouting stuff at me. **Not nice stuff.** All except Chewy. He's just wiping sauce off himself and off the kids around him with his sausage rolls and **chomping** into them.

Right beside me is Meredith Murdoch. Her glasses have a fat line of red plastered across them and it's **dribbling** down her nose and cheeks. But I can still feel her eyes **burning** into me. Then she yells out ...

TUESDAY: I accidentally leave the lid off our class ant farm after I was on roster to feed them. It wouldn't have been quite so bad if Clayton Whitman-Byrnes hadn't brought his fancy cupcake display for Show and Tell that day. Clayton wants to be on **Junior Master Chef.** I think he'll make it, too, because those cupcakes must have been **really delicious.** Judging by how much the ants liked them.

ERIC VALE - EPIC FAIL!

WEDNESDAY: Somehow Mrs. Booth in the library gets me mixed up with some girl in Year One called **Erin Dale,** and when she's reading the overdue books out over the intercom **for the entire school to hear,** she says, "Eric Vale. Year Five. You have two books overdue: Baby Wu Wu's Adventure and Ducky Takes a Waddle!"

ERIC VALE - EPIC FAIL!

THURSDAY: I think I've survived the day without a disaster! **Yippee!** Then we have a Drama class in the last lesson and we have to act out a scene from a movie. Chewy and I are put in a group with Macie Hudson and Sasha Bronski. We want to do something from **X—Men.** The girls want to do something from **Harry Potter.** The girls win. As usual. I have to play Harry Potter. Chewy has to play Dobby the house elf because the girls reckon Chewy looks "just like him!" I'm not sure this is a good thing. It could be the ears. And his size. And everything else about him.

Anyway, Macie Hudson draws a big **lightning bolt** on my forehead and round glasses on my face with a washable marker pen. I look **stupid.**

Then when the bell goes for the end of the day we discover that of course Macie picked up the wrong pen! Yes, it's the **permanent** one. So I have to ride home in the bus painted up like a stupid boy wizard. Everyone laughs. Lots of people ask me if I'm looking for Platform 9 ¾. And I get challenged to about a hundred games of quidditch. They think it's hilarious.

ERIC VALE - EPIC FAIL!

FRIDAY: I'm playing soccer before school. I'm a defender. The ball comes bouncing to me and because I don't want to have any epic fails, I take a big kick at it to clear it right away from my team's goal. But I miskick it completely and it heads for our classroom. It's going straight at a window!

I put my hands over my ears waiting for the big crash. But it goes right through without a sound because the window is open! **YEEEESSS!** Thank you! A minor epic win! My luck is definitely changing at last!

I run into our classroom. There's a bunch of girls standing around a desk. On the desk is a big cake. Or what's left of a big cake. It must have been a birthday cake, but it's hard to tell because it's been **completely smashed** like a bomb has gone off inside it. But I can see a bit on the floor with "HAPP" written on it in red icing.

And then I see another bit with "SOP" on it. That bit is **squished** on the front of a dress. Inside that dress is Sophie Peters. She doesn't look like she's having a very happy birthday.

Then I notice that Sophie Peters is holding a soccer ball. My soccer ball! It's covered in cake and cream. So is Sophie Peters. So is Li Wan. So are all the other girls. The only one not covered with **gobs** of cake and cream is Aasha Alsufi. That's because she's sitting way down the back of the classroom by herself. I smile at her. But she stares at me the same way as the other girls are. Like I'm a **cake murderer!**

Sophie Peters is **way** too nice to say it,
but I know exactly what she's thinking.

ERIC VALE - EPIC FAIL!

LOOSER

Name: ~~Eric Vale~~ FAIL
Favourite Subject: ~~English~~ EPIC FAILING
Favourite Superhero: ~~Batman~~ BOZO THE CLOWN
Future Career: ~~Writer~~ WRONGER

And then, just to top off the week
perfectly, on Friday afternoon when I'm
packing my bag to finally go home, I see the
picture I drew of myself at the beginning
of the year for our **Who Am I?** unit. It's
pinned up on the noticeboard with everyone
else's. But it's looking **worse** than
Chewy's self-pootrait.

Someone's drawn a big "L" on my forehead
and given me clown hair and a clown nose.

→ 125 ←

They've also written "Loser" on my shirt. Except they spelled it "**Looser.**" Which is kind of funny when you think about it. But I wasn't smiling.

I pulled it down, scrunched it up and threw it in the bin. If only it was that easy to get rid of my **stupid nickname!**

HA! FAIL.

o•o•o•o•o•o•o•o•o•o•o•

Every spare minute I had on that weekend I spent imagining myself beating Martin Fassbender in the freestyle final at the school swimming carnival on Monday.

Positive thinking for positive results!

FIRST

(WHO CARES)

On Sunday night I started getting really **nervous.** The next day was supposed to be the scene of my epic win. But a swimming carnival was like a school assembly — just the sort of place where, if you weren't really careful, you could actually end up having the **epic-est** of all epic fails.

At least I had one thing going for me. On the day I'd get to wear my brand new **super-cool** swimmers! Mum had gone shopping and she'd finally bought the ones I'd been bugging her about for ages. They were shiny and white with little **skulls** on them and yellow **lightning flashes** down the side. Super-cool!

OOH! THOSE ARE REALLY UNCOOL!

Of course Mum also went and bought me some teeshirts that weren't quite so cool. But they ended up being **super-awesome** compared to the pyjamas she got for me, which were the least cool thing in the **entire universe.** Can you believe that the top had **Sweet Dreams!** written on the front in tiny kisses? And the shorts were white with little teddy bears all over them!

"Well, they were an absolute bargain, sweetie – sixty per cent off! – **and** I thought they'd look so **cuuuuute** on you. Besides, who's going to ever see them?"

60% OFF
WORST IN THE UNIVERSE SPECIAL

Hello, Mum! Have you noticed I'm not in a crib any more and I actually go to the toilet **all by myself?** Sometimes mums just don't get it. She even made me try them on, but then I just left them on the kitchen table.

UGH. I DON'T FEEL LIKE EATING.

But freaky pyjamas weren't my problem. My problem was the next day's swimming carnival and all the things that could go wrong for me there. I knew I had to be **totally** prepared. Like the big sign above Chewy's desk says, "If you FAIL to PREPARE, you are PREPARING to FAIL!"

I prepared this table:

(kidding)
turn
over

Possible Epic Fail situations.

1. I dive into the pool for the big race and my new super-cool swimmers come off.

2. I'm standing in front of the whole school and as a stupid joke stupid Martin Fassbender pulls my new super-cool swimmers down to my ankles.

3. I sit out in the sun all day and get so sunburnt and dehydrated that I pass out and fall into the pool and almost drown and old Mrs. Winklebottom who's always in charge of first aid and whose teeth wobble and click when she talks has to give me the kiss of life. Eeeeewwwwwwww!

Precautions to take.

Tie new super-cool swimmers up with special DOUBLE knot.

Tie new super-cool swimmers up with special super-tight TRIPLE knot!

Wear a HAT and cover every inch of my body with multiple layers of 30+ SUNSCREEN*.

* Make sure I have one tube of blue sunscreen (my team colour) to paint war stripes on my face and one tube of clear sunscreen for everywhere else.

4. I run along the pool deck, slip over, hit my head, knock myself out, fall into the pool and almost drown and then just when you thought it was safe to go back in the water ...
ATTACK OF THE WINKLEBOTTOM!!

5. I have breakfast and eat way too much and during the big race I get stomach cramps and almost drown and it's —
WINKLEBOTTOM 2 — REVENGE OF THE DENTURES!!!!

6. I stay up so late worrying about all the epic fails that might happen at the carnival that I sleep in and I'm still half asleep when I have to rush to get dressed and when I get to the carnival I realise that I've left my new super-cool swimmers at home and I'm wearing my underpants on the outside of my shorts.

Absolutely NO RUNNING on the pool deck!

Have breakfast EARLY and don't eat so much!

Get everything ready, pack bag and put clothes out BEFORE I go to bed. Set the alarm for six o'clock. Wear my new super-cool swimmers to school UNDER my shorts to save time getting changed and so I can't possibly forget them.

By the time I'd finished drawing up my table and preparing everything for the morning it was getting late and I was pretty tired. I jumped into bed and turned off the light. I'd covered every possibility.

Nothing could go wrong!

As I lay there with my eyes closed, I pictured myself **slicing** through the water in my new super-cool swimmers and leaving Martin and everyone else for **dead.** I could see myself flying down the pool. I was certain to **win!** No more epic fails for this Eric Vale! Time for an epic ...

BEEEWAAAH!
BEEEWAAAH!
BEEEWAAAH!
BEEEWAAAH!
BEEEWAAAH!
BEEEWAAAH!

6:00 AM

My alarm goes off. It's six o'clock **already!** It's still mostly dark. I hit the **snooze button** and roll out of bed. I'm half asleep but I've run through my preparations so many times in my head that I know **exactly** what I have to do without even thinking.

First I use the bathroom. Then I return to my room. I feel around for my new super-cool swimmers. I find them right where they should be – on the back of my desk chair where I left them last night. I strip off and put them on straightaway. **No chance** of leaving them behind now! Then I tighten the drawstring and do it up with a special super-tight triple bow. Then I decide to give it **one more knot** for good measure. I grab the sides of my swimmers and yank down as hard as I can. Those babies aren't going anywhere fast! I'm leaving **nothing to chance.** Already I'm feeling more relaxed!

Next I pull my sport shorts on over my new super-cool swimmers. Then I **fumble** around my desk and find a tube of sunscreen and start to **smear** it on. I can hardly keep my eyes open. I've covered my whole face and neck before I switch on my small desk light and lean close to the mirror.

EEEEEEEEEEEK!

One of those Avatar guys is staring back at me! I've been using the blue sunscreen by mistake! Wait. Doesn't matter. And you know why? Because it actually looks **really** good. It makes me look like a true Blue supporter. My teammates will love it. Hey, what about that? I've had a tiny win already! Things are really looking up! This is going to be **my day!**

CLIK!

EYWA!

I leave my face blue and **attack** the rest of my body with the clear stuff. I go over **every square inch** at least three times. I almost **dislocate** my arms and tie myself into **a knot** trying to do my back, but I don't miss a spot. When I'm done I finish getting dressed and jam on my hat. No **sunstroke** for me!

My bag is already packed from the night before so I take it into the kitchen and fix myself some breakfast. When I'm finished I rest my head on the bench.

Half an hour later **I wake up** when Mum comes out to make my lunch. I drag my head up.

"Huh? What time is it?"

"Just past seven, sweetie. AWWWWWWWWWWW, look! You're all blue! That is so **cuuuute!** You're still my gorgeous little Smurf boy, aren't you?"

I run to the bathroom and scrub off all the blue sunscreen and replace it with clear stuff. Back in the kitchen I shove my lunch into my bag and kiss Mum goodbye. She makes a big **dopey** sad face and pretends to wipe tears from her eyes when she sees I've been de-Smurfed. I shake my head at her.

It's time to go and I'm spot on schedule!

I'd done everything right. I was feeling epic fail-proof. All I had to do now was beat Martin Fassbender at the annual Moreton Hill Primary School Swimming Carnival. I was thinking **super positive** for **super positive** results!

The time had come for Eric Vale to have the **EPIC-EST-OF ALL EPIC WINS!**

Epic Fail No. 8:

The Annual Moreton Hill Primary School Swimming Carnival

For the first time the swimming carnival was held in our brand new school pool (partly built by a kind donation to the school building fund by the **fascinating,** entertaining, **enthralling** and **totally hilarious** Deputy Mayor Doreen Dorrington on behalf of the Council).

All of Years Four to Seven were packed in and divided into team colours. Red and Green on one side. Gold and Blue on the other. Chewy was in Blue, just like me.

There were quite a few events for the younger kids before our call came over the loudspeaker.

> Could all Year Fives get changed immediately and assemble behind the starting blocks in your correct divisions.

The divisions had all been worked out at our class swimming lessons. Luckily I'd made the **first division. Just.** So had Martin. **Easily.**

Chewy and I were in the dressing shed with the other Year Fives getting changed. I was about to take off my school shorts.

"Hey, Chewy," I say, "how **SUPER-cool** are these?"

Then I whip off my sport shorts to show him my new super-cool swimmers. I watch Chewy's face. His mouth drops open. His eyes go big. He's obviously **impressed!**

"Wow! They're **different,** all right, Eric," he says. Then he leans closer and squints. "Are they ... teddy bears?"

"Yeah that's right, pretty coo–"

Huh? What? I looked down to where my new super-cool swimmers should be. But for some reason I'm not wearing my new super-cool swimmers. I'm wearing my **humungously** and **stupendously UNCOOL** teddy bear pyjama bottoms! But? ... What? ... How?

NOOOOOOOOOOOOOOOO! IT'S
JUST NOT POSSIBLE!

(Unless of course ... my mum brought
my new pyjamas into my room while I was
asleep and she hung them on the back
of my chair right **ON TOP** of my
super-cool swimmers and then when I woke
up in the morning I just grabbed whatever
was there because it was dark and I was half
asleep and so I put my teddy bear pyjamas on
instead of my new super-cool swimmers
by mistake. Hmmmmm. Yeah. Yeah, when I think
about it, I guess **that's** possible.)

WAAAAAAAAAAAAAAAAAHHHHHHH!

I whip a towel around myself before anyone
else has a chance to see what I'm wearing. I wait
till the other Year Fives leave and Chewy and I
are alone.

"Chewy, you gotta help me! What am I going to do? If I swim in these I'll be Eric Vale — Epic Fail for the rest of my life!"

"Don't you like them?"

"OF COURSE I DON'T LIKE THEM! THEY'RE PYJAMAS! THEY'VE GOT TEDDY BEARS ON THEM! NO WAY AM I SWIMMING IN THEM! WHAT AM I GOING TO DO?"

"Hey, you could swim in your underpants!"

"Oh yes! **Awesome idea!** Me, standing up on the blocks of the first division final ... in my underpants. Why didn't I think of that?

MAN, THESE ARE SOME BIG UNDERPANTS.

That would be sooooooo much better, wouldn't it? Or wait, I know. I'll wear my undies on my head as a swimming cap and just swim nude! Thanks, Chewy. Problem solved!"

I was starting to **panic.** Outside I could hear Year Fives being called again over the loudspeakers. I needed to **calm down** and think this through.

STICK-ON LEAVES

Okay then. Let's see. Hmmmm, I wonder what Secret Agent Derek "Danger" Dale would do in a situation like this?

Hey, I know! I'll knit myself a pair of swimmers out of my own bellybutton fluff!

That's when I knew I was losing it completely. I looked madly around the change room for something – **anything!** – that could help.

And then ... *I SAW IT!*

The lost property bag! It was hanging over in the corner of the shed. I grabbed it and tipped everything out. Towels. One thong. Goggles. A cap. A mouldy half-eaten sandwich. Three startled cockroaches. AND TWO PAIRS OF SWIMMERS!

One pair was way too small but the other looked right around my size. SAVED! I held them up to show Chewy.

"All right!" I shouted and we gave each other a high five.

HEY, MY SHORTS!

At last I was going to be free of my embarrassing teddy bear pyjamas! Or I **would** be ... if I could ... juuuuuuuuust ... undo ... this ... stupid ... **quadruple knot!**

GRRRRRRRRRRRRRRR!

I started yanking and picking and scratching at it, but it just got smaller and tighter! Then I tried **squeezing** and **wiggling** out of the pyjama bottoms while Chewy yanked down on them. But those babies weren't going anywhere!

"Hey, maybe I can **bite** that knot off," Chewy said, coming at me with his pointy teeth like something out of **Alien.**

"AAAAAAAAAAAAAAAAAAAH! GET AWAY FROM ME, YOU MANIAC!"

Last call for any competitors from Year Five. Report immediately to Mrs. McGurk. If you are not lined up in your correct division behind the starting blocks in one minute you will not be swimming!

I threw a towel around my waist. "Let's go," I said to Chewy. "I'll figure something out when we get there!"

And I did. While I was lined up waiting for my race I came up with **a plan** that even Secret Agent Derek "Danger" Dale would be proud of.

o•o•o•o•o•o•o•o•o•o•o•o•

There were six divisions in our age group. First division was swimming **last.**

Chewy was in the **bottom** division. But naturally he acted like he was in the final of the World Swimming Championships. He didn't seem to notice that he was in a race that included Big Bob, one swimmer who was starting in the pool, two boys with kickboards, and another kid wearing **floaties.** The starter was Mr. Heatherington. He was sitting on a tall starter's chair on the side of the pool. When the whistle blew, Chewy climbed up on his block and **saluted** the crowd. He was at least a head shorter than everyone else in the race and about three heads shorter than Big Bob. He started twisting his neck from side to side and shaking his legs and arms to loosen his muscles **(what muscles?).**

MUSCLE
COMING
LOOSE

He was wearing a proper swimming cap and bright yellow racing goggles. He looked like a real swimmer.

Until you saw him swim.

Mr. Heatherington waited for everyone to settle. "Take your blocks ... Face the water ... GO!"

The six starters jumped, dived, climbed, fell, **bellyflopped** and pushed off into the pool. Big Bob's entry caused a **tsunami** that washed two swimmers on to their lane ropes and the floaties guy right up on to the pool deck and out of the race! Chewy's diving technique looked a lot like someone getting shot in the back, falling face first into the water and then getting **electrocuted.**

As soon as his fingers touched the surface of the water, Chewy's arms and legs started thrashing around in circles like some kind of **nuclear-powered** wind-up toy. Then, if he had to take a breath, he stopped completely, lifted his head right out of the water, made a noise like a **dying sea lion** and slapped it back in again. Then the nuclear-powered thrashing began again until the next breath. All of which meant that Chewy didn't swim too fast. Or too straight.

Right from the start he motored his way across the pool at an angle of about forty-five degrees.

GRORFLE!

He thrashed his way right over a dividing rope and **collided** with one of the kickboard swimmers in the lane beside him. For a few seconds there was a tangle of arms and legs but Chewy easily **out-thrashed** the other boy. He also out-kicked his kickboard, which went flying from the pool. The kickboard-less kid sank to the bottom. A Year Seven on lifeguard duty jumped in to rescue him.

But a little speed bump like that was never going to stop William Choo-Choo Rodriguez in full flight. He just kept going until he ploughed into the other kickboard guy just as he was lifting up his head for one of his dying sea lion breaths.

POW!

Chewy's head connected with the kickboard boy's nose. It started **bleeding.** The kickboard kid let go of the kickboard, grabbed his face and started **sinking.** More Year Sevens to the rescue!

But Chewy thrashed on! **Eventually** he **slammed** into the side of the pool, thought he'd finished first and gave **a victory salute.** When he realised where he was, he bounced off in the opposite direction, swam right over Big Bob's back, got beached there for a while then crawled off and **nosedived** back into the water.

He ended up coming third. Mainly because only three other swimmers survived the race.

The rest of the school gave Chewy a standing ovation and chanted, "Woo-hoo! Choo-Choo! Woo-hoo! Choo-Choo!" Chewy collected his Third Place ribbon and walked proudly back to the starting blocks grinning and waving to everyone like he'd just taken out Olympic Gold. And in his **positive thinking** brain, he probably thought it was only a matter of time.

But now I had to put my plan into action.

"Okay, Chewy," I said when he made it back to the starting blocks, "you sure you know **exactly** what you have to do here?"

"Yeah, I'm all over it, Eric."

"You **sure?** This is **really** important to me. I don't want anything to go wrong."

"I'm sure. I stand behind you when you're on the block. I hold on to the end of your towel. You dive in and the towel stays with me and you're under the water before anyone sees what you're wearing. Then I run down to the finish with the towel and wrap you up as you get out. And everyone goes **so crazy** because you beat Martin that they don't notice a thing. And that's how you have your **epic win** and nobody calls you Epic Fail any more."

"Okay."

Well, I said it was a plan that Secret Agent Derek "Danger" Dale would be proud of. I didn't say anyone else would be.

I HEARTILY ENDORSE THIS PLAN!

When all the lower divisions were done it was finally time for the Year Five first division final. I took my place behind the blocks. I was in the outside lane.

"Eric Vale, you're not thinking of swimming in that towel, are you?"

It was Mrs. McGurk, my old Year Four teacher.

"Ah, no, Miss."

"Well, get rid of it, then!"

Oh-oh. **Big problemo ...**

"Aaah ... I can't, Miss. Not now."

"Why ever not?"

"Because ... um ... my mother said I had to keep it on ... until I got in the water ... Ah, that's right ... See, I got my legs all **sunburnt** at ummm ... swimming practice ... Yeah, and so Mum said I had to keep my legs covered 'at all times.' They were her exact words, Mrs. McGurk, 'at all times.' I reckon she'd be **pretty** upset if I didn't do what she said. Can't I just give Chewy, I mean, William, my towel right before I dive in?"

Mrs. McGurk looked at me **suspiciously.** I'm not sure if she believed me or not, but I don't think she wanted another argument with my mother. Not after last year's parent-teacher interview anyway. She signalled to Mr. Heatherington that we were ready.

WHY ME?

"Hey, Vale!" It was Martin Fassbender from the middle lane. "You're right on the edge there. When you dive in, make sure to aim at the water. Wouldn't want you to do an Eric Fail face-plant on the concrete!"

Soooooo funny. Well, **laugh it up,** pal. After this race you'll never be able to make another Eric Fail joke ever again!

The whistle blew.

"Take your blocks!"

I stepped up. Chewy was close behind me. I felt his hand grab on to the edge of my towel. So far so good! There was a lot of murmuring and looking around in the stands. I guess everyone was wondering what was going on. Mr. Heatherington **frowned** at Mrs. McGurk. She just shook her head and waved him on. He shrugged.

"Face the water!" YAAAAAAA!

I knew I couldn't afford to break. I couldn't
have a restart. I only wanted to climb out
of the pool in my teddy bear pyjamas once.
I bent forward and waited ... and waited ...
and waaaaaaaaaiteeeeeeeed ... Why was
Mr. Heatherington taking so lo ...

"GO!"

I launched myself forward. I hadn't
broken and I'd still beaten everyone
else into the water. **BRILLIANT!**

I resurfaced and started swimming
my heart out. I could hear good old Chewy
running along beside me on the pool deck
screaming out encouragement,
"Go, Eric! Go, Eric! Go!" I remembered all

the things Mr. Heatherington told me about my strokes and my kicking. I was **powering** through the pool. The swimmers beside me fell away like they'd stopped **dead!**

The race was only half over and already I was well in the lead. **I was flying!** The school was going **nuts**. I could hear **yelling** and **screaming.** The finish was just metres away.

"Go, Eric! Go, Eric! Go!"

One Eric Vale Epic Win coming up!

I slapped my hand hard against the end of the pool. I raised both arms above my head and pumped my fists in **victory.**

I shook the water from my ears.

"NO, ERIC! NO, ERIC! NO!"

Huh? What?

I looked across the pool. I was still the only one at the finish line. Wow. I didn't think I'd win by **that** much. I spun round in the water. All the rest of the guys were at the other end. A couple had just climbed out of the pool. Three were still on the blocks. One of them was Martin. He was holding his stomach and doubled over laughing. A lot of people in the stands were doing the same thing. I spun back round to Chewy.

"What happened?"

"It was a false start."

Eric Vale, please return to the starting blocks.

"False start? What do you mean, false start? It couldn't have been! I was the first one in the water and my feet were still on the block when Heatherington said **Go.**"

"That's the thing, Eric. Heatherington didn't say **Go.**"

"What do you mean, Heatherington didn't say **Go?** Of **course** he did. I heard him. I heard him loud and clear."

"No – see that's where you made your mistake."

"My mistake?"

"Yeah. That was **me** you heard."

"YOU? YOU! What did **you** say **Go** for?"

"Well, Mr. Heatherington was taking such a long time, I thought he must've forgotten that bit. So ... I just did it for him."

"You ... did it ... for him ..."

I couldn't believe it. My mouth was moving but no words were coming out.

"Real shame too," Chewy said. "I reckon you would have won **easily** if you didn't muck up the start."

"Wha ..."

ERIC VALE, IF YOU DON'T RETURN TO THE STARTING BLOCKS IMMEDIATELY, YOU WILL BE DISQUALIFIED!

"Okay, forget it! Just give me my towel."

Chewy gazed down to his empty hands ... then around his feet ... and then back to the other end of the pool. He frowned. "Your towel? Oh, yeah ... that's right. I was supposed to bring that with me, wasn't I?"

"ERIC VALE!"

There was nothing else I could do. If I was going to save myself from a **lifetime** of Eric Vale – Epic Fails I just **had** to beat Martin now, no matter what I was wearing. I dragged myself out of the pool and stood up.

The stands were filled with people laughing, **hooting,** pointing, **whistling** and shouting out. Even some of the teachers were calling out to me. Some example they were setting! I tried to block it all from my mind.

"Talk about **childish!**"

Chewy nodded.

"Just because I **happen** to be wearing some stupid pyjamas."

Chewy nodded again.

"And because they **happen** to have a few stupid teddy bears on them."

Chewy nodded for a third time and added, "And I **guess** because they **are** pretty see–through when they're wet."

I nodded this time.

"Yeah, there's that, I suppo ..."

Wait a minute? **WHAT? WHAT!**

I glanced down.

NOOOOOOOO! CENSORED

I ripped Chewy's swimming cap off his head and covered whatever bits of myself I could. The change rooms were down at the far end of the pool behind the starting blocks. I had to get there – **FAST!**

I set off at warp speed. Straightaway Principal Porter's voice blasted through the loudspeakers beside me.

NO RUNNING ON THE POOL DECK!

I freaked out. I jammed on the brakes. Or tried to. But the side of the pool was wet and smooth and as slippery as ice, so instead of stopping, my feet kept right on going. They **rocketed** off the tiles and took off into the air like **two jet fighters.** (Hey, I bet that's why they don't like people running on the pool deck!) I landed with a thump on my back.

OOOMF!

My three layers of greasy sunscreen hit the super-slippery tiles and I **zoomed** along the pool deck like a **human bowling ball!**

TORO!

The next person I saw was Mr. Winter. He was running towards me waving a towel. When he realised we were on a collision course he leapt out of the way and accidentally shoulder-charged Mr. Heatherington and his tall starter's chair into the pool. I flashed past them. There was nothing I could do! I couldn't stop! I was a human bowling ball with turbo thrust! A human bowling ball with turbo thrust that was now heading ... right ... for ...

THE OFFICIALS' TABLE!

STRRRIIIIIKE!

I scored a **direct hit** on the legs of the long folding table where the judges were sitting. One end of the table crashed down and the other end shot up.

For a few seconds the table, along with assorted pens, pencils, sheets of paper, staplers, laptops, microphones, drinks, boxes of ribbons, sandwiches, salad rolls and a few teachers became airborne.

And then they came back down.

On top of me.

I ended up **buried alive** under a tangle of arms and legs – some human, some belonging to chairs and tables – and an **avalanche** of stationery, electrical equipment, food and ribbons! Mainly ribbons.

A whole boxful must have landed on my head. They were stuck to every inch of my greasy triple–sunscreen–layered body. I'd been turned into **a human piñata!**

Then someone started pulling stuff off me. Three faces appeared. Which was **weird,** because all the faces belonged to William Rodriguez. They were all **fuzzy** around the edges and bobbing around everywhere. I closed my eyes and gave my head a shake. When I opened my eyes the three Chewy heads had melted into a single blurry one.

"Wow, Eric. Far out. Are you all right?"

But before I could answer him, Chewy reached forward and peeled a ribbon from my forehead. An excited smile spread over his face.

"Hey, Eric, look. You got a **First Place!** Cool!"

I was beginning to feel **dizzy** again when I heard a different voice.

"Stand well back, everyone! Give me some room here! The boy needs **first aid!**"

Chewy's blurry face disappeared and another one took its place. It floated closer.

"Hmmmmm, doesn't look good," said a giant mouth filled with wobbly, clicking teeth. "He **might** require resuscitation."

SOMEBODY SAVE ME! I WAS ABOUT TO BE WINKLEBOTTOMED!

It was supposed to be my epic win, but the swimming carnival turned into the epic-est of all my epic fails! **I was doomed!** The only good thing was that when I saw Mrs. Winklebottom's face in **close-up,** I got **such a fright** that my head cleared completely and I didn't need the **slobber of death** after all. PHEW!

Afterwards when I was in the change room recovering, Mr. Winter said, if I wanted to, I could sit out the rest of the carnival back in the classroom. I WANTED TO! A LOT! So when Chewy brought my bag in, I cut off the quadruple knot with scissors from the first aid kit and got changed. Then while everyone was busy cheering for some big relay race, I **sneaked back** up to our homeroom.

It was **weird** sitting in the classroom all alone. All I could think of was how **bad** it was going to be when everyone else came back from the carnival. For sure Martin and Tyrone would have these big, **stupid grins** on their faces and they'd be going on about "Eric Vale — Epic Fail," and the rest of my class — except for my **crazy best friend** — would either be laughing at me or looking at me like I was a **total loser.**

I wanted to stop myself thinking about that so I opened my bag and dragged out my special **Awesome Stories and Genius Thoughts Journal.** I thought maybe that would help. I read over the last thing I'd written about Derek "Danger" Dale. I had him in **a heap of trouble** again ...

Agent Dale stared up at the fifty-tonne block of granite hanging right above him. The cable holding it was snapping one bit at a time.

Now it was down to its last thin strand! With his arms and legs staked to the hot sand and his body weakened by a deadly paralysing drug, it seemed to Derek that this time, there was no way out.

Making up Derek Dale adventures always took my mind off stuff and cheered me up. I found my pen and wrote some more ...

And what do you know? Secret Agent Derek "Danger" Dale was absolutely right. There was no way out.

> **OW!**

The cable snapped and the giant granite block dropped and squished him totally to mush!

Yeah, well, **that** didn't work!

I groaned and did a Mr. Winter. I thumped my head three times on the desk. I was still groaning and moaning with my head on the desk when I heard someone else in the room. I thought it might be Mr. Winter. I looked up. Someone else **was** in the room, all right. But it wasn't Mr. Winter.

It was Aasha Alsufi. Mr. Winter let her miss the carnival because she was **really frightened** of water.

← **WATER**

→ 173 ←

Her big, dark eyes were **staring** at me. I stared back with my **puny** green ones. She was standing just inside the door holding a book. I figured she must have come from the library. Our **stare-a-thon** had been going on for quite a while, so I thought I'd better say something. But then she beat me to it.

I sat up straight. I couldn't believe it. The new girl was speaking! She was using actual words! But her voice was so soft. I didn't hear her properly.

"Sorry, what?"

She spoke again. This time I heard the words. They were plain and clear. And very familiar.

FAIL FAIL FAIL FAIL

FAIL

FAIL

"Epic fail," she said.
Well, that's **just great!**
Everyone's been knocking themselves out,
competing against each other for the
grand prize of being the **big**
hero who gets the new girl to talk, and
then, when she finally opens her mouth for
the first time, she's calling me names! After
my teddy bear pyjamas **disaster,**
this was just **too much!**

"Yeah, you're right," I told her. "You
absolutely got it in one. That's me. Good
old **stupid** Eric Vale, the good old
stupid Epic Fail! Go on. Have a big
belly laugh, why don't you? Might as well.
Everybody else has today. Wouldn't want
you to be the only one to miss out on all
the fun."

FAIL

FAIL

FAIL

FAIL

FAIL FAIL FAIL

FAIL FAIL

Aasha Alsufi frowned. Hard. She shook her head. A lot. Then her big brown eyes moved from me to the direction of the swimming pool and back again.

"Epic fail?" she said again.

That's when I finally got it. She wasn't **calling** me Epic Fail. She was **asking** me if I'd **had** an epic fail down at the carnival. Well, there was only one answer to that.

"Totally! Completely! Absolutely!" I told her.

"The epic-est of all epic fails. The epic fail that makes all other epic fails look like wins. The **Godzilla** of epic fails! It's quite a story. I'd tell you all about it, but you wouldn't believe me."

EEEEK! I GRABBED THE WRONG SHORTS!

AIM FOR THE PYJAMAS!

I thumped my head back down on the desk and stayed there. A moment or two later I heard a chair scrape. I looked up. Aasha Alsufi was sitting right in front of me. She was holding her library book on her lap. She raised her eyebrows at me and her big eyes got **even bigger.**

"I like stories," she said.

And because there was nothing else I could do, and because Aasha Alsufi turned out to be a really, **really** good listener, I told her everything. I told her all about Big Bob and the big plan to beat Martin, about my super-cool new swimmers and my super-uncool teddy bear pyjamas, about the quadruple knot and all my other preparations for the carnival, about Chewy and the false start, and finally about how I climbed out of the pool in front of the whole school.

"And when I get out of the water," I said, "everyone goes **totally nutso.** And you wanna know **why everyone** goes totally nutso?"

Aasha looked a bit **unsure** at first, **but then** her head bounced up and down.

So I reached into my bag and pulled out my teddy bear pyjama shorts. They were still wet.

I held them up in front of her.

Aasha Alsufi's big eyes looked like they were **about to explode.** She clamped both hands over her mouth and kept them there while I told her about me running down the pool deck, turning into the human bowling ball and **wiping out** Mr. Winter, Mr. Heatherington and the entire Officials' Table.

NUTSO

"See what I mean? **The Big Momma** of Epic Fails!"

I squeezed my eyes shut and tried to block it all out of my mind.

But then I started hearing a **strange** noise. A squeaky, sniffling, snorty kind of noise. I opened my eyes. Aasha's hands were still clamped over her mouth. But she was looking kind of **weird.** Her eyes were all wrinkled up and I thought that maybe she was about to cry or even be **sick.** But then her shoulders started shaking and I worked it out. She was trying to **stop** herself from laughing!

She was doing a pretty good job, too, until **a big burst** of air squeezed between her lips and fingers.

It made a noise on its way through.

A noise that sounded like a giant **you-know-what.**

Aasha Alsufi dropped her hands from her mouth and laughed out loud. She laughed and laughed till she had little tears in her eyes.

I laughed too. I couldn't help myself.

"I don't know what you think is so funny," I told her when we'd both calmed down a bit and we were trying to suck in some deep breaths. "You wait. I bet you see-through teddy bear pyjamas will be **all the rage** at the beach this summer!"

And that started us both off all over again. We were laughing so much we didn't even notice that Mr. Winter and the rest of the class had arrived back from the carnival and were crowded in at the front of the room **gawking** at us.

When Aasha saw them, she got **a huge fright** and her face changed. It looked the same as it did that first day when she came into our classroom. Then her head dropped and she stared down hard at her library book. She was holding on to it like it was **a lifejacket.** But it didn't look like it was ever going to be enough to save her.

I really wanted to help. But what could I do? Where was Secret Agent Derek "Danger" Dale when you needed him? In the end, I just said the first thing that came into my head.

"Aasha really likes stories," I told them. "Especially **weird** ones about

SORRY WHAT WAS THAT?

epic fails and see-through teddy bear pyjamas."

Mr. Winter and the rest of the class stopped gawking when I said that. Then they started **grinning** and **laughing.** Even Martin and Tyrone had stupid smiles on their faces – but in a good way.

The noise made Aasha look up. At first when she saw everyone smiling at her, she **froze.** But then, slowly, bit by bit, she began to smile back. As we watched, Aasha Alsufi's smile just kept growing and growing.

And it didn't stop growing till it looked big enough to swallow the entire room.

MEGA, AWESOME, EPIC WIN!

o•o•o•o•o•o•o•o•o•o•o•o•o

That night I added two more entries to my **Awesome Stories and Genius Thoughts Journal.**

One was this:

A big cloud of dust rose around the fifty-tonne block of granite.

"Aha! At last I have finally destroyed that slimy pest, Secret Agent Derek 'Danger' Dale, forever! He's been flattened into a pancake of squishy mush. The world is mine! Mine, I tell you!"

"Not so fast, evil Doctor Evil MacEvilness."

Agent Dale strolled out from behind the concrete block brushing dirt from his chest and straightening a stray hair on his forehead.

MacEvilness's face turned purple with anger.

"But ... but how did you escape? You were paralysed and pinned to the ground and a fifty-tonne block of granite landed RIGHT ON TOP OF YOU! I saw it with my own eyes! No one could find a way to escape that! It's impossible! COMPLETELY IMPOSSIBLE!"

Secret Agent Derek "Danger" Dale just smiled and twirled something between his fingers.

"Impossible, MacEvilness?" he said. "I think you'll find that nothing is impossible with a wad of bellybutton fluff and a bit of POSITIVE THINKING!"

And the other entry? Well, **that** was my first ever **Genius Thought.** It went like this:

"Just because you have some epic fails in your life, it doesn't mean you are one."

I reckon Chewy's mum and dad should put that in their next book!

(What's next for Eric Vale? Will he be **up for sale, on the trail** or something even more **off the scale?** Wait and see. Coming soon.)